Dawn the Deer

Dave and Pat Sargent are longtime residents of Prairie Grove, Arkansas. Dave, a fourth-generation dairy farmer, began writing in early December 1990, and Pat, a former teacher, began writing shortly after. They enjoy the outdoors and have a real love for animals.

Dawn the Deer

By

Dave and Pat Sargent

Illustrated by
Jean Lirley Huff

Ozark Publishing, Inc.
P.O. Box 228
Prairie Grove, AR 72753

Library of Congress Cataloging-in-Publication Data

Sargent, Dave, 1941-
    Dawn the deer / Dave and Pat Sargent ; illus-
trated by Jeane Huff.
       p. cm. — (Animal pride series ; 8)
    Summary: Farmer John comes to the rescue
when a faun becomes separated from   her mother. Includes facts about the physical characteristics,
behavior, habitat, and predators of the deer.
    ISBN 1-56763-013-8. — ISBN (invalid) 1-
56763-088-4 (alk. paper)
    1. Deer—Juvenile fiction. [1. Deer—Fiction.]
I. Sargent, Pat, 1936- .
    II. Huff, Jean, ill. III. Title. IV. Series:
Sargent, Dave, 1941- Animal pride series ; 8.
    PZ10.3.S243Daw   1996
    [Fic]—dc20
    96-1492
    CIP
    AC

Printed in the United States of America

iv

Inspired by

the beauty and grace with which deer move, and their big, beautiful, trusting eyes.

Dedicated to

our granddaughter, Ashley Kay Sargent Corrales, who has great big, beautiful brown eyes, and to all those who could never fire a shot.

Foreword

Asleep in the tall grass, Dawn is awakened by a hound passing by. She is so startled that she jumps up and runs to the other side of the farm. Lost and hungry, Dawn calls for her mother, but Mama Sue is on the other side of the farm frantically searching for Dawn. Suddenly, a tractor and mowing machine pull into the field where Dawn is hiding.

Contents

Dawn the Deer

If you would like to have the authors of the Animal Pride Series visit your school, free of charge, call 1-800-321-5671 or 1-800-960-3876.

One

Dawn

It was now early May and the weather was nice and warm. All the does had given birth. Mama Sue had a little girl fawn. She named her Dawn.

Dawn was a pale, light brown with white spots all over. When she was first born, she tried to stand, but her small, weak, wobbly legs would not support her weight.

Dawn kept trying to get up and, after fifteen minutes or so, she had all four legs under her and was standing alone. She was doing fine until she tried to walk. Her legs gave way and she fell to the ground.

Dawn kept getting up and kept trying to walk. It was a good thirty minutes before she was able to get some warm, fresh, first milk from her mother. That first milk would give her instant strength, which would help her walk, then run and jump.

Dawn was born at the crack of dawn (the very first sign of light in early morning). That's why her mother had named her Dawn. By midday, she was able to run like the wind. Mama Sue stayed with Dawn all day the first day.

That first night, Mama Sue moved Dawn to some tall grass in the middle of Farmer John's field. She said, "Lie very quiet, Dawn, and go to sleep. I'll be sleeping nearby. I'll wake you in the morning, just as soon as it gets light."

The next morning, just as the darkness started to give way to the light, Mama Sue woke Dawn and fed her some warm milk. After Dawn was full of milk, Mama Sue said, "Dawn, you lie back down and wait right here until I get back. Now don't worry, for I will not be far away. I'll be back when the sun is halfway across the sky."

Dawn said, "Okay, Mama," and laid down in the tall grass.

Dawn was only one day old and her mother knew that she would spend most of her time sleeping. By the time the sun was high in the sky Dawn was awake and hungry.

When Mama Sue showed up,

Dawn jumped to her feet and started nursing. She was really hungry and Mama Sue's warm milk tasted good.

Every night Mama Sue moved Dawn to a new place in the field to sleep. She did this to help keep wild animals like wolves and coyotes from finding her.

After Dawn was a week old, she was awake most of the time. One morning just before sunup, Mama Sue moved Dawn to another new place in the field. She said, "Dawn, wait right here. I'll be back before dark."

Dawn was now old enough that she would get milk only twice a day. She nursed just after daylight, and just before dark in the evening.

It was mid-morning and Ole Barney the Bear Killer was out for his morning stroll. He was checking the farm over to make sure no varmints were eating Farmer John's crops or bothering his beehives or any of his animals.

As Barney strolled through the tall grass, he walked right by Dawn. He stopped and gazed down at her.

When Dawn looked up and saw Barney, she jumped to her feet, let out a loud bleat, and took off across the field just as fast as her little legs would carry her! She had never seen anything like Barney before, and she was very scared.

Barney had gotten the name *"Bear Killer"* because he had once killed a mean ole grizzly bear who had turned *killer*. It had wandered onto the farm and started killing and eating Farmer John's baby calves before Barney stopped it cold.

Even though Barney was both respected and feared just a little bit by some of the animals, he wasn't really that bad. Why, ole Barney would never bother young animals. He would never hurt a baby animal in any way. And that was a fact.

Now, ole Barney figured that Dawn's mother would find her when she returned that night. But Barney didn't know just how scared Dawn was and how far she would run.

Baby Dawn didn't quit running until she was on the other side of Farmer John's place. When she was too exhausted to take another step, she lay down in the tall grass to wait for her mother.

The sun was sinking below the horizon when Mama Sue came back to the grassy field to feed Dawn her evening milk. Dawn was not where she had left her. She looked all around, then said, "Now, where could that little fawn be?"

Mama Sue bleated softly, again and again, but could hear no answer. She searched the pasture over. She kept bleating for Dawn. The bleats were getting louder, for Mama Sue was worried. Yet, she heard nothing that sounded like a baby deer in trouble.

Mama Sue searched for Dawn all night. The next morning, when the sun was high in the sky, she gave up. She left the field, fearing Dawn was gone forever. For she had smelled ole Barney the Bear Killer's tracks all over the field, and she just knew that he had eaten her baby.

Two

Farmer John Finds Dawn

Dawn was awake on the other side of the farm and was very, very hungry. She said, "I wonder where Mama is? I wonder why she doesn't come feed me? I'll bet that big ole thing that was after me, got Mama."

Dawn called for her mama by making a little bleating sound. She called and called, but her mother didn't answer. Mama Sue never came.

Dawn lay back down in the tall grass and, with an empty stomach, went back to sleep.

The sun was hot that day and Dawn was getting weak. Since babies can't go very long without food, Dawn wouldn't last long.

That afternoon, right after lunch, Farmer John started cutting the tall grass in the meadow where Dawn was sleeping. Now, when she heard the noisy tractor coming, she lay as still and quiet as she could, hoping that whatever the thing was wouldn't find her.

Just before sundown the noise suddenly stopped. Dawn waited for several minutes, then began bleating for her mama. She called and called, but Mama Sue didn't answer.

The next morning Farmer John walked through the meadow where Dawn was. He was heading for his tractor to finish cutting the tall grass.

He heard a baby deer bleating. He stopped and listened. He knew by the sound that the little deer was lost and hungry.

Farmer John said, "I'd better look for the young deer." And, after a time, he saw her. She was standing in some tall grass, bleating for her mama. Farmer John could tell by looking at her that she hadn't eaten in a long time.

Dawn was so weak, she could hardly stand. Farmer John had no problem catching her. He took her to his house and had his daughters feed her. Their names were Amber, April, and Ashley. Amber was eight, April was five, and Ashley was almost two. The girls took one of Ashley's bottles that she had used when she was a baby, and filled it with warm milk. While Amber held Dawn, April forced the nipple into Dawn's mouth. Once Dawn tasted the milk, she sucked the bottle dry.

Farmer John said, "I reckon that's enough for now. You girls can feed her again tonight."

Farmer John fixed a pen for baby Dawn in the back yard. He built a small house so she would have shelter from the rain.

He told Amber and April, "It will be your job to feed the little deer every morning, and every evening. Ashley is too young to help, but she'll have to go to the pen with you so she can watch and learn about caring for the baby deer."

Every time Amber and April fed Dawn, she wanted more. They knew that if they fed her too much she would get sick.

After the first day, the girls let Dawn out of her pen. She followed them around like a little puppy dog.

That evening, when coming in from the field, Farmer John saw a deer searching the field down past the barn. He felt sure that it was the fawn's mother looking for her.

Farmer John watched the deer for several minutes, then decided to try and get them back together. He went on to the house and told the girls, "The little fawn's mother is searching the field, looking for her baby. I'm going to take her out back of the barn, near her mother, and turn her loose."

The girls were sad about Dawn leaving, but they knew it was for the best. She belonged in the woods with her mother.

Three

Mama Sue Finds Dawn

Farmer John took Dawn to the field where he had seen the mama deer. As he neared the top of a small rise he saw the mother deer at the far side of the field. He sat Dawn on the ground and began making sounds like a young deer bleating. He watched very carefully to see if the mother deer would answer the calls, and sure enough, Mama Sue raised her head, then began making her way toward Farmer John.

Farmer John turned and started toward the house, but young Dawn followed him. He tried to get her to stay and wait for her mama, but is was no use. Dawn had gotten used to Farmer John and the girls and had accepted them as her family.

Farmer John finally went back to the house with Dawn right behind him every step of the way.

Mama Sue was still making her way to where she had heard the bleating sounds. Once she got there, she smelled Dawn's scent and knew her little fawn had been there, but where was she now? Mama Sue searched and searched but it was no use. She finally bedded down for the night in the tall grass.

The next morning Farmer John went to the field where he had seen the mother deer. He looked the field over, but there was no sign of her. He went on to the meadow and cut hay all day. Just as he was quitting, he stood up and slowly searched the field with his eyes. He saw a female deer on the other side of the farm.

On the way home, Farmer John tried to think of a way to get Dawn and her mother back together.

When he got to his house, he looked for a large box. When he found one, he took his pocketknife out of his pocket and cut the top out of the box. Then he cut several small holes in the four sides.

Farmer John took the box and Dawn to the field where he had seen Mama Sue. When he got to the edge of the field, he was very careful not to make any noise. He didn't want to scare Mama Sue away.

Farmer John moved ever so slowly until he could see Mama Sue. He set Dawn on the ground and placed the box with the holes in it over her. He then placed two small rocks on top of the box.

Farmer John moved back a short ways and once again made bleating sounds like a young deer. Mama Sue raised her head and looked all around.

Farmer John again made the bleating sounds. Mama Sue turned and started in his direction. He moved back into the edge of the woods and waited.

Mama Sue slowly made her way toward Dawn. When she got close enough to see the box, she stopped. She turned her head sideways. She wasn't sure about the box.

She started walking a wide circle around the box, and once she got downwind, she could smell Dawn. She slowly made her way toward the box.

Farmer John hoped that young Dawn's mama would find her baby under the box, turn it over, and set her free. But Mama Sue was afraid of the box and wouldn't get very close.

It started getting dark, and Farmer John could no longer see the big box with the hole in the side or Mama Sue. There was nothing to do but leave Dawn under the box until morning.

The next morning at first light, Farmer John finished milking the cows then hurried to the field to check on the baby deer. The box had been turned over and the little deer was gone. Farmer John didn't know if the baby deer's mama had turned the box over and set her free or if a varmint had gotten her.

That evening, just after sun down, Farmer John saw Mama Sue strolling across the field. And right behind her, running, jumping, and playing, was Dawn. Farmer John called to Amber, April, and Ashley.

The girls ran out of the house just in time to see Dawn disappear into the edge of the woods. A smile covered their faces as they shed tears of joy, for they knew Dawn was safe, and at home with her mother.

Four

Deer Facts

Deer are the only animals with bones called antlers on their heads. Antlers are true bones, unlike horns, which are strong, hard layers of skin.

Antlers grow from permanent knob-like bones on the deer's skull. Deer use their antlers chiefly to fight for mates or for leadership of the herd. Among most species of deer, only the males have antlers, but both male and female reindeer and male and female caribou have them. The musk deer of Asia and the Chinese water deer do not have antlers.

Deer that live in mild or cold climates always lose their antlers each winter. New ones begin to grow early the next summer. Deer that live in warm or hot climates may lose their antlers and grow new ones at other times of the year.

New antlers are soft and tender. Thin skin grows over the antlers as they develop. Short, fine hairs on this skin make it look like velvet.

Full-grown antlers are hard and strong. The velvety skin dries up, and the deer rubs the dry skin off by scraping its antlers on the ground or against trees or bushes. The antlers fall off several months later. They usually decay on the ground or are gnawed by small animals.

The size and shape of a deer's antlers depend on the animal's age and its health. The first set grows when the deer is one to two years old. On most deer, these first antlers are short and somewhat straight. The antlers grow longer and larger and form branches.

Almost all male deer are called bucks. But male caribou, elk, and moose are called bulls, and male red deer are called stags or harts.

Most female deer are called does. But female caribou, elk, and moose are cows, and female red deer are called hinds.

A female deer chooses a hidden spot away from other deer to give birth to her young. The young deer remain in their hiding place until they can walk well enough to follow the mother.

Most young deer are called fawns, but young caribou, elk, and moose are called calves.

Fawns of white-tailed deer weigh from three and a half to six pounds at birth. They stay hidden for four or five weeks.

Newborn moose calves weigh about twenty-five to thirty pounds. They can follow their mother when they are about ten days old.

Caribou calves, most of which are born during the herd's spring migration, weigh about ten pounds at birth. They can walk with the herd several hours later.

Most kinds of deer have only one or two young at a time. Chinese water deer, which live along the Yangtze River, give birth to the most young--four to seven fawns at a time.

There are more than sixty kinds of deer, including elk, caribou, moose, musk deer, reindeer, and white-tailed deer. Deer live in many parts of the world.

Deer are among the largest wild

animals of North America. The North American moose is the largest deer in the world. Some grow seven and a half feet tall and weigh over eighteen hundred pounds. The smallest deer is the pudu of South America. It is about one foot high and weighs about twenty pounds.

People use deer meat for food and deer skins for clothing. The Indians taught the pioneers how to dry venison (deer meat) in the sun or over a campfire. This is called jerking. It makes the meat light weight. People could carry large amounts easily, and keep it for later use.

All deer have long, thin legs. They run on their tiptoes. Powerful muscles in the upper part of the legs allow the animals to run swiftly and to take long jumps. A frightened white-tailed deer can run as fast as forty miles per hour, and can leap fifteen to twenty feet. Even the huge, clumsy-looking moose can run about twenty miles per hour.

There are more than sixty kinds of deer. The best known deer is the white-tailed deer of North America.